The Jew's Beech

The Jew's Beech

Annette von Droste-Hülshoff

Translated by
Lionel and Doris Thomas

ALMA CLASSICS

ALMA CLASSICS
an imprint of

ALMA BOOKS LTD
Thornton House
Thornton Road
Wimbledon Village
London SW19 4NG
United Kingdom
almaclassics.com

The Jew's Beech first published in 1842
Translation © John Calder (Publishers) Limited, 1958
First published in this translation from the German in 1958 by John
Calder (Publishers) Limited
This edition first published by Alma Classics in 2008. Repr. three times.
This revised edition first published by Alma Classics in 2024

Cover: David Wardle

Printed in Great Britain by CPI Group (UK) Ltd, Croydon CR0 4YY

ISBN: 978-1-84749-918-9

Contents

The Jew's Beech

Introduction

Annette von Droste-Hülshoff was born on 10th January, 1797, at Hülshoff, near Münster, both her parents being members of the Westphalian nobility and of the Roman Catholic Church. A premature child, she never enjoyed robust health. From her father's family she inherited musical talent and an appreciation of all aspects of Nature; from her mother's, the von Haxthausens, whose estates lay in the Paderborn district, both her gift of literary composition and that virility of expression which is one of her most striking characteristics. The dominating personality of Annette's mother, who never gave unqualified approval to the publication of her daughter's works, engendered a somewhat narrow-minded and strictly conventional attitude to social and religious questions within the family circle; to counteract this, Annette deliberately sought the acquaintance of those with wider cultural interests. When her brothers were taught

3

by private tutors, she shared their education, which included languages, history, natural science, music and mathematics – a subject for which she showed unusual aptitude. Her mother directed that the works of great writers like Shakespeare, Cervantes, Voltaire, Swift and Scott should be read to her children, and here the foundations of Annette's admiration and understanding of British authors were laid; later she was to enthuse over Byron, and, during the period when *The Jew's Beech* was being composed, she reread Scott with greater insight. Her knowledge of Latin was useful to her, particularly when she began to collect and classify stones, coins and fossils. Her first known poem dates from 1804, but it is unlikely that she received encouragement in her literary pursuits until she was fifteen, from which time she was guided by Matthias Sprickmann, a minor writer of an earlier age. One of her main interests during these years was the collecting of folk songs and fairy tales. Her youth was spent within the boundaries of Westphalia; only from 1818 onwards did she venture further afield, mostly to the Rhine or Lake Constance. Despite her nobility of birth, she became intimately acquainted with the common folk of her homeland, even sharing their superstitious beliefs in ghosts and second sight. Much of her work bears witness to her shrewd observation both of the natural beauties of Westphalia and of the characteristics of its people. In 1819 she met two young men, August von Arnswaldt and Heinrich Straube, to both of whom she felt drawn; as a result of some kind of misunderstanding, she lost both potential suitors. Her survival of this experience without lasting bitterness may be partly attributed to her religious faith, to which she now turned for consolation, writing a number of poems – the first of the cycle *The Church's Year* (begun in 1820, continued and completed in 1839) – in which her doubts and questioning are sometimes reflected.

After the move to Rüschhaus in 1826, Annette's life became still more secluded, despite occasional visits to Münster. In 1830 she met Levin Schücking, who was to be her only link with contemporary literature. Although he was seventeen years younger than her and never felt any stronger affection for her than that of friendship, her feelings towards him, though apparently maternal or sisterly, were more intense. Their literary association inspired Annette to further composition. In the few months between the autumn of 1841 and the spring of 1842, when both were staying with Annette's sister and brother-in-law at Meersburg on Lake Constance, the Annette wrote fifty of her best poems, many of them embodying reminiscences of her beloved Westphalia. This group represents a considerable proportion of her output of lyric poems and ballads. Schücking later arranged for the publication of *The Jew's Beech* in 1842. After he had left Meersburg, the friendship between the two writers cooled, partly because Annette was out of sympathy with the social and political trends of the literature of the day for which her younger friend showed increasing interest. As the years passed and her health declined, she spent ever more time in Meersburg, settling there in 1846. It was here that she died on 24th May 1848. Although she recognized that her work was unseasonable during her own lifetime, she hoped that it might be appreciated fifty years after her death. This wish was largely fulfilled when it came into its own with the Naturalists at the end of the century, and since that time Annette von Droste-Hülshoff has enjoyed a position of merited pre-eminence among the greatest woman writers and poets of Germany.

The Jew's Beech

A PICTURE OF LIFE AMONG THE HILLS OF WESTPHALIA

Where is the hand so fraught with gentle art
That tangled skein of narrow mind may part,
So steadfast that untrembling it may throw
The stone upon a wretched creature's woe?
Who dares to measure surge of vain ambition,
To ponder prejudice, the soul's perdition,
To weigh each word which, still retained,
Its power o'er youthful heart has gained?
Thou happy man, thou being born in light,
Cherished and guided piously towards right,
Judgement is not thy task, lay scales aside!
Take up no stone – lest it towards thee should glide!

Born in 1738, Friedrich Mergel was the only son of a small farmer or freeholder of the humbler kind in the village of B***, which, despite its smoky and poorly constructed buildings, caught the traveller's eye because of the picturesque beauty of its situation in a green forest glen among an imposing range of hills remarkable for their historical associations. The province to which it belonged was then one of those remote areas without industry, commerce or main roads where a strange face still created a sensation and a journey of a hundred miles made even a man of rank the local Ulysses – in short, a place once common in Germany, and with all the faults and virtues, all the eccentricity and narrow-mindedness that can only flourish under such conditions.

As a result of primitive and often inadequate legislature, the ideas of the inhabitants as to right and wrong had become somewhat confused, or rather beside the official legal system there had grown up a second law based on public opinion, usage and superannuation arising from neglect. The landowners, who had the privileges of magistrates in the courts of petty sessions, punished or rewarded in accordance with motives which were honest for the most part; the peasants acted as seemed feasible and compatible with a somewhat elastic interpretation of what could be reconciled with conscience, and it only occurred sometimes to the loser in a lawsuit to consult the ancient and dusty records.

It is difficult to view that time impartially, for since its passing either arrogant censure or fatuous praise have been bestowed on it, while the witness who has first-hand experience is blinded by too many familiar memories and the later generation is not capable of comprehending it. This much may be said, however: legal form mattered less, the spirit was adhered to more strictly, infringements occurred more often, but complete unscrupulousness was rarer. For a person who acts according to his convictions, however imperfect they may be, can never perish entirely, whereas nothing destroys the soul more surely than an appeal to external legal forms in contradiction to one's inner sense of justice.

Many of the actions of the inhabitants, a race more restless and enterprising than their neighbours, attained far greater prominence in the little country of which we are speaking than they would have done elsewhere in similar circumstances. Violation of the forest and game laws was the order of the day, and, since brawls often took place, everyone had to console himself as best he could for a broken head. However, since the chief wealth of the country lay in the extensive and profitable woodlands, the timber was carefully patrolled, but less by lawful means than by continually renewed attempts to overcome violence and cunning with the same weapons.

The inhabitants of B*** were reputed to be the most stiff-necked, wily and spirited community in the whole principality. The situation of the village, secluded amidst dense, proud forests, may have nourished early their inborn stubbornness of temperament; the vicinity of a river flowing to the sea and bearing covered barges large enough to carry timber for shipbuilding conveniently and safely out of the country did much to stimulate the natural boldness of the timber thieves. It was merely an incentive to them that the district was swarming with foresters, for in the skirmishes which frequently occurred the advantage usually lay with the peasants. On fine, moonlit nights thirty or forty carts set out together, carrying about twice that number of persons of every age from the half-grown youth to the seventy-year-old headman, who, as an experienced ringleader, led the procession with as much conscious pride as he displayed taking his seat in the courtroom. Those who remained behind listened without anxiety as the noise of the wheels creaking and jolting down the glen gradually died away, then they calmly resumed their slumbers. It is true that an occasional shot or feeble cry sometimes caused a young woman, married or betrothed, to start up in her sleep, but no one else took any notice. With the first light of dawn the procession returned home as silently as it had departed; faces glowed like bronze; here and there a bandaged head was to be seen, but this was a matter of no account, and a few hours later everyone in the district was talking about a mishap to one or more of the foresters, who were carried out of the woods battered, bruised, blinded by snuff and unable to perform their duties for some time.

It was in this environment that Friedrich Mergel was born, in a house which, boasting a chimney and window panes rather larger than usual, testified to the pretensions of its builder, while its dilapidated state indicated the miserable circumstances of the present owner. The wooden railings which had formerly encircled garden and yard had given way to a neglected fence; the roof was defective; the cattle grazing on the pastures and the corn growing on the land adjoining the yard did not belong to the owner – and, apart from a few gnarled rose trees, relics of a better time, the garden contained more weeds than cultivated plants. Admittedly misfortune had been responsible for much of this, but considerable disorder and bad management had also played their part. As a bachelor Friedrich's father, old Hermann Mergel, had been a so-called "regular" drinker, that is one who only lay in the gutter on Sundays and feast days, while he was as respectable as anyone else throughout the week. Thus he found no difficulty in courting a girl who was both handsome and well-to-do. They had a merry time of it at the wedding. Mergel was not too badly drunk, and in the evening the bride's parents went home in good spirits. On the following Sunday, however, the young wife was seen running through the village to her people, screaming, covered in blood, abandoning all her new household utensils. That was indeed a great scandal and vexation for Mergel, who was badly in need of consolation. Thus it was to be expected that by the afternoon not a window pane in his house should be still intact, and that, till late into the night, he should be seen lying in front of his door, raising a broken bottleneck to his lips from time to time and woefully cutting hands and face. The young wife stayed with her parents, until she soon pined away and died. Whether it was remorse or shame which now tormented Mergel, suffice it to say that he seemed ever more in need of a source of consolation and was soon numbered among those who had gone irretrievably to the dogs.

House and farm fell into decay; hired maids brought it loss and discredit, as the years passed. Mergel was, and remained, a lazy widower living in rather poor circumstances, until he suddenly appeared once more as a bridegroom. If the event itself was unexpected, the character of the bride caused even greater astonishment. Margret Semmler was an honest, decent woman in her forties, who had been a village beauty in her youth and was still respected for her shrewdness and thrift; at the same time, she was not without means of her own, and thus nobody could understand what had driven her to this step. We believe that the motive for her action lay in that very consciousness of her own perfection. On the evening before the wedding ceremony, she is said to have declared: "A woman who is ill treated by her husband is stupid or worthless. If I live to regret it, say it's my own fault." What followed unfortunately showed that she had overestimated her powers. At first she overawed her husband; whenever he had drunk too freely, he did not come home or crawled into the barn; but the yoke was too heavy to be borne long, and soon he was to be seen often enough staggering across the road into the house, making a deafening noise inside so that Margret hurriedly closed doors and windows. On one such evening – now no longer a Sunday – she was seen rushing out of the house without cap or neckerchief, her hair hanging wildly about her head; she threw herself down in the garden beside a vegetable bed and dug up the earth with her bare hands. Then, looking fearfully about her, she quickly gathered a bundle of herbs and went back slowly towards the house with them, finally entering not the house, but the barn. Although a confession never passed her lips, it was said that Mergel had first laid hands on her that day.

The second year of this unhappy union saw the birth of a son – one cannot say it was gladdened by it, for Margret is believed to have wept a great deal when the child was handed to her. However, although borne under a heart full of grief, Friedrich was a healthy, handsome child who thrived in the fresh air. His father was very fond of him and never came home without bringing him a piece of fine wheaten bread or something of the kind, and people were even of the opinion that he had grown steadier since the birth of the child – at least there was less noise in the house.

Friedrich was now eight years old. It was a cold stormy winter night around the time of Epiphany. Hermann had gone to a wedding, having started early, because the house of the bride was about four miles away. Although he had promised to come back in the evening, Frau Mergel was not counting on this, particularly since a dense snowstorm had set in after sunset. Towards ten o'clock she raked the ashes together on the hearth and prepared to go to bed. Friedrich, already half undressed, stood beside her, listening to the howling of the wind and the rattling of the window in the loft.

"Mother, isn't Father coming home tonight?" he asked.

"No, child, tomorrow."

"But why not, Mother? He promised."

"Goodness, if he kept all his promises! Get along with you, off to bed."

They had scarcely lain down when a gale arose, threatening to sweep the house away. The bedstead shook, and there was a rattling in the chimney as though a goblin were there.

"Mother – there's someone knocking outside!"

"Quiet, Fritz, that's the loose board on the gable blown by the wind."

"No, Mother, at the door!"

"It doesn't close properly, the latch is broken. Goodness, go to sleep! Don't rob me of the little rest I get at night."

"But supposing Father comes now?"

His mother turned violently in the bed.

"The Devil will look after him!"

"Where is the Devil, Mother?"

"Just wait, you fidget! He's at the door and will fetch you if you don't be quiet!"

Friedrich fell silent, listened for a short while longer and then went to sleep. He awoke a few hours later. The wind had turned and now hissed like a snake past his ear through the crack in the window. His shoulder had grown numb with cold, and, in his fear, he crept deeper under the cover and lay quite still. After some time he noticed that his mother too was not sleeping. He heard her weeping and praying, at intervals, "Hail, Mary!" and "Pray for us sinners!" The beads of the rosary slid past his face, and he was unable to suppress a sigh.

"Are you awake, Friedrich?"

"Yes, Mother."

"Pray a little, child, that God may keep us from flood and fire. You already know half the Lord's Prayer."

Friedrich thought of the Devil and what he might look like. The many different sounds and noises in the house seemed strange to him. He thought there must be something alive, both inside and outside.

"Listen, Mother – isn't that someone knocking?"

"No, child, but there's no old board in the house that isn't rattling!"

"Listen! Don't you hear? Someone's calling! Listen!"

His mother sat up in bed. When the raging of the storm abated for an instant, a knocking at the window shutters and the sound of several voices could be heard distinctly.

"Margret, Frau Margret! Hey, open up!"

Margret uttered a violent cry. "They're bringing me back the swine again!"

The rosary flew rattling onto the yarn winder; clothes were snatched up. She ran to the hearth, and soon afterwards Friedrich heard her striding defiantly over the threshing floor. Margret never came back to bed, but in the kitchen there was much murmuring and the sound of strange voices. Twice an unknown man came into the room and seemed anxious to find something. Suddenly a lamp was brought in, followed by two men supporting his mother. She was as white as chalk, and her eyes were closed. Friedrich thought she was dead; he gave a fearful scream, whereupon someone boxed his ears; this quietened him, and now he gradually realized from what was said by those around him that his father had been found dead in the wood by Uncle Franz Semmler and Hülsmeyer and was now lying in the kitchen.

As soon as Margret regained consciousness, she tried to get rid of the strangers present. Her brother stayed with her, and Friedrich, threatened with severe punishment if he left the bed, heard the whole night through the fire crackling in the kitchen and a noise like scuffling of feet and brushing. Little was spoken, and that softly, but sometimes the boy could hear sighs which, young as he was, went to the very marrow of his bones. At one point he understood his uncle to say: "Margret, don't take on so – we'll each have three masses said for his soul, and at Easter we'll make a pilgrimage to the Mother of God at Werl."

When, two days later, the body was taken away, Margret sat by the hearth, covering her face with her apron. After a few minutes, when all was quiet once more, she muttered to herself: "Ten years, every one a cross. Yet we bore them together, and now I am alone." Then she said louder: "Come here, Fritz!" Friedrich approached shyly; his mother seemed alien to him in her black ribbons and with her troubled expression. "Fritz," she said, "are you going to be good now and make me happy, or are you going to be wicked and tell lies or drink and steal?"

"Hülsmeyer steals, Mother."

"Hülsmeyer? God forbid! Do I have to whip you? Who tells you such wicked stories?"

"Not long ago he beat Aaron and took sixpence from him."

"If he took money from Aaron, the wretched Jew had certainly swindled him out of it earlier. Hülsmeyer is a respectable man, one of us, and Jews are all rogues."

"But, Mother, Brandis too says that he steals wood and game."

"Child, Brandis is a forester."

"Mother, do foresters tell lies?"

Margret was silent for a while, then she said: "Listen, Fritz, God makes wood grow in freedom, and the game changes its haunts from the land of one master to that of another – it can't belong to anybody. But you can't understand that yet – now go to the shed and fetch firewood for me."

Friedrich had seen his father lying on straw, where, it was said, he had looked blue in the face, a terrible sight. However, he never spoke of it, and seemed unwilling even to think of it. The memory of his father had left in him a tenderness mixed with horror, for nothing is so captivating as love and care from a person who seems hardened against everything else, and with the years this feeling grew through the sense of many a slight suffered from others. Throughout his childhood he was extremely sensitive to any allusion to the dead man phrased in none too praiseworthy terms, an unhappiness not spared him by any consideration on the part of the neighbours. In those districts it is the customary belief that victims of disaster enjoy no rest in the grave. Old Mergel had become the ghost of Brede Wood. In the form of a will-o'-the-wisp he had almost led a drunken man into Zelle Pond. The shepherd boys, whenever they huddled over their fires at night and the owls hooted in the glens, sometimes heard quite distinctly in the intervals the disconnected notes of his song – 'Listen, pretty Lizzie' – and an unauthorized woodcutter who had fallen asleep under the Broad Oak as night had come on had, on awakening, seen his swollen blue face peeping through the branches. Friedrich had to hear a good deal about this from other boys, whereupon he howled, struck out at those around him, sometimes stabbed at his enemies with his little knife, and was lamentably beaten on these occasions. Since that time he drove his mother's cows alone to the other end of the valley, where he was often to be seen lying in the grass for hours on end in the same position and plucking the thyme from the ground.

He was twelve years old when his mother received a visit from her younger brother, who lived in Brede and had not crossed her threshold since her foolish marriage. Simon Semmler was a small, restless, spare man with bulging, fish-like eyes and a face just like a pike's – an eerie fellow in whom pompous reserve often alternated with a candour just as affected. He fancied himself as a man of enlightenment, but was reckoned to be a malicious trouble-seeker whom everyone preferred to avoid, the more as he approached an age at which men who are in any case limited in intelligence easily gain in pretensions what they lose in usefulness. However, Margret, who had no other relatives still alive, was pleased to see him.

"Is that you, Simon?" she said, trembling so much that she had to hold on to a chair. "Have you come to see how I and my grubby boy are getting on?"

Simon looked at her earnestly and held out his hand. "You have grown old, Margret!"

Margret sighed. "Since you saw me last, I've often had a bitter time of it, with all kinds of misfortunes."

"Yes, my girl, marry too late and repent ever after! Now you are old and the child still small: everything has its own time, but when an old house catches fire, there's no use in trying to put it out."

A flame, red as blood, shot across Margret's careworn face.

"But I hear that your boy is sly and smart," Simon continued.

"Yes, he is rather, but he is pious too."

"Hm, there was once a chap who stole a cow – he was also called Pius. But he is quiet and thoughtful, isn't he? He doesn't run around with other boys?"

"He's an odd child," Margret said, as though to herself. "That isn't a good thing."

Simon burst into a hearty laugh. "Your boy is shy because the others have tanned his hide a few times; he'll pay them back all right. A little while ago Hülsmeyer was at my place, and he said, 'Friedrich is as nimble as a deer.'"

What mother's heart is not gladdened, when she hears her child praised? Poor Margret had seldom felt so happy. Everyone else called her boy artful and sulky. The tears started to her eyes. "Yes, he has straight limbs, thank God."

"What does he look like?" Simon went on.

"He has much of you in him, Simon, very much."

Simon laughed. "Well, he must be a fine fellow, for I get handsomer every day. He must be careful not to get his fingers burnt at school. Do you make him mind the cows? That's just as good as going to school. Not half of what the schoolmaster says is true. But where does he mind the cows, in Telge Glen or in Rode Wood? In the Teutoburg forest? Nights too and early in the morning?"

"Whole nights through – but why do you ask?"

Simon seemed not to hear her question; he stretched his neck towards the door. "Well, here comes the lad! He's the son of his father and swings his arms just like your dead husband. And just look! The boy really has my fair hair!"

A fleeting smile of pride lit up the mother's features; the fair curls of her Friedrich compared with Simon's ginger bristles! Without answering, she broke off a branch in a nearby hedge and went to meet her son, apparently to drive on a lazy cow, but really to whisper to him a few quick, half-threatening words, for she knew his stubborn nature, and Simon's manner had seemed to her today more intimidating than ever. But all went far better than she had expected: Friedrich was neither stubborn nor insolent in his behaviour, but rather somewhat bashful and very eager to please his uncle. Thus it happened that, after a half-hour's talk, Simon proposed a kind of adoption of the boy, by which he would not deprive his mother of him completely, but would have him at his disposal for the greater part of the time, in return for which he was to inherit the old bachelor's possessions (these would certainly have come to him in any case). Patiently Margret listened to the explanation of how much she would stand to gain, how little to lose through the bargain. She knew best how much an ailing widow would miss the help of a twelve-year-old son whom she had already trained to take the place of a daughter. Yet she kept silent and gave way in every respect. She only begged her brother to be strict but not hard in his treatment of the boy.

"He is a good lad," she said, "but I'm a lonely woman, and my son is not like one ruled by a father's hand."

Simon nodded slyly. "Just leave it to me, we'll soon get along. I'll tell you what – let me have the boy straight away. I have to fetch two sacks from the mill; the smallest is just right for him, and he'll learn to lend a hand. Come, Fritz, put on your clogs!"

And soon Margret was looking after them both as they walked away, Simon in front, cleaving the air with his face, while the tails of his red coat trailed behind him like flames of fire. Thus he looked rather like a "fiery man" atoning for his guilt beneath his stolen sack, Friedrich following him, slim and well made for his years, with delicate, almost noble features and long fair curls which were better cared for than one might otherwise have expected from his appearance. For the rest he looked ragged, sunburnt and neglected, while his expression reflected a certain rude melancholy. Nevertheless one could not fail to recognize a great family likeness between them, and, as Friedrich thus walked slowly after his leader, his gaze firmly fixed on his uncle, who attracted him just because of the strangeness of his appearance, he called to mind someone who regards with troubled concentration the image of his future in a magic mirror.

Now they both approached the place in the Teutoburg forest where Brede Wood stretches down the side of the mountain and covers a very dark ravine. Up to this point little had been said. Simon seemed thoughtful, the boy absent-minded, and both panted under their sacks. Suddenly Simon asked: "Do you like brandy?" The boy did not reply. "I'm asking if you like brandy. Does Mother sometimes give you some?"

"Mother herself has none," said Friedrich.

"Really? All the better! Do you recognize that wood in front of us?"

"That is Brede Wood."

"And do you know what happened there?"

Friedrich was silent. Meanwhile, they drew ever nearer to the gloomy ravine.

"Does your mother still pray so much?" Simon went on.

"Yes, two rosaries every night."

"Really? And you pray with her?"

With a knowing look, the boy laughed, half embarrassed by the question. "Mother prays one rosary at dusk before supper – I'm usually still away with the cows then – and the other in bed when I mostly fall asleep."

"Really, my lad?"

These last words were spoken under the shade of a wide-spreading beech which arched over the entrance to the ravine. It was now quite dark; the first quarter of the moon was in the sky, but its faint gleams only served to give a weird appearance to the objects on which they sometimes shone through a gap in the branches. Friedrich, breathing quickly, kept close behind his uncle, and, if anyone had been able to see his face, he would have noticed the expression of an intense excitement which was more the result of imagination than real fear. Both strode on vigorously, Simon with the firm tread of the hardened walker, Friedrich staggering and as if in a dream. It seemed to him as though everything were moving, the trees, lit up by occasional moonbeams, swaying sometimes together, sometimes one away from the other. Tree roots and slippery places, where water had collected on the path, made his steps uncertain. At times he nearly fell. Now, some distance away, the darkness seemed to part, and soon they stepped into a fairly large clearing. The bright moonlight showed that only recently the axe had raged here pitilessly. Everywhere tree stumps projected, many several feet above the ground, just as they could be cut most conveniently by somebody in a hurry; the furtive labour must have been interrupted unexpectedly, for a beech in full leaf lay right across the path, its branches stretching high above, its foliage, still fresh, trembling in the night wind. Simon stopped for a moment and regarded the felled trunk attentively. In the middle of the clearing stood an old oak, broad rather than high; a pale beam, falling through the branches onto its trunk, revealed that it was hollow – this was probably why it had been preserved from the general destruction. At this point Simon suddenly grasped the boy's arm.

"Friedrich, do you recognize the tree? That is the Broad Oak." Friedrich started and clung with cold hands to his uncle. "Look," Simon went on, "here Uncle Franz and Hülsmeyer found your father, after he had gone to the Devil in his drunkenness without confession and extreme unction."

"Uncle, Uncle!" gasped Friedrich.

"What's the matter? Surely you are not afraid? You're pinching my arm, you young devil! Let go! Let go!" He tried to shake off the boy. "Otherwise your father was a good chap and God won't be too hard on him. I loved him like my own brother."

Friedrich let go of the arm of his uncle; both went in silence through the rest of the wood, and then Brede village lay before them, with its clay huts and the few better houses of brick, of which Simon's home was one.

The next evening, Margret had already been sitting with her distaff for an hour in front of the door, waiting for her boy. It was the first night that she had spent without hearing the breathing of her son beside her, and Friedrich still did not come. She was annoyed and anxious, and knew that it was without reason. The clock in the tower struck seven; the cattle returned home; he was still not back, and she had to get up to look after the cows. When she entered the dark kitchen, Friedrich was standing by the hearth; he had bent forwards and was warming his hands at the coals. The firelight played on his features and gave them a repulsive appearance, stressing their leanness and nervous twitching. Margret stopped at the door of the threshing floor, so strangely altered did the boy seem to her.

"Friedrich, how is your uncle?" The boy muttered inaudibly and pressed close to the chimney. "Friedrich, have you lost your tongue? Speak up, boy! You know that I'm deaf in my right ear." The boy raised his voice and began to stammer so violently that Margret understood no better than before. "What are you saying? Master Semmler sends his greetings? Gone away again? Where to? The cows are already home. Wretched boy, I can't understand you. Wait, let's see if you still have a tongue in your head!"

She advanced a few quick steps towards him. The boy looked up at her with the woeful glance of a wretched, half-grown creature being trained as a watchdog, and in his fear began to stamp his feet and rub his back against the chimney.

With an anxious glance, Margret halted. The boy seemed shrunken to her, even his clothes were not the same – no, that wasn't her child! And yet... "Friedrich, Friedrich!" she cried.

A cupboard door banged in the bedroom, and the summoned boy stepped forward, in one hand a so-called "Holschen fiddle", that is an old clog with three or four frayed violin strings stretched over it, in the other a bow equally battered. He went straight up to his stunted double with a bearing of conscious dignity and independence, which at this moment threw into bold relief the difference between two boys who were otherwise remarkably alike.

"There you are, Johannes!" he said, and handed him that work of art with the air of a patron. "There is the violin I promised you. I must give up playing now that I must earn money." Johannes darted another shy glance at Margret, then slowly stretched out his hand, until he had firmly grasped what was offered him and slipped it as though in stealth beneath the flaps of his shabby jacket.

Margret stood quite still and did not interfere. Her thoughts had taken another far more serious turn, and she looked restlessly from one to the other. The strange boy had bent over the coals again with an expression of momentary bliss which bordered on idiocy, while Friedrich's features reflected an interest patently more selfish than good-natured, and his eyes revealed for the first time, in their almost glass-like clarity, the unbridled ambition and inclination to give himself airs which afterwards appeared as such a strong motive for most of his actions. A call from his mother wrenched him away from thoughts which were as novel as they were pleasant to him. She was sitting again at the spinning wheel.

"Friedrich," she said hesitantly, "tell me…" and then fell silent. Friedrich looked up and, when he heard nothing further, turned back to his protégé.

"No, listen…" she said, and then, more softly:

"Who is that boy? What's his name?"

Friedrich answered just as softly: "That's Uncle Simon's swineherd, and he's taking a message for Hülsmeyer. Uncle gave me a pair of shoes and a canvas waistcoat which the boy carried for me on the way; in return I promised him my violin. He's only a poor lad – he's called Johannes."

"Well?" said Margret.

"What do you want, Mother?"

"What's his other name?"

"No other name… but wait a minute… yes… it's Niemand* – he's called Johannes Niemand… he hasn't got a father," he added in an undertone.

Margret stood up and went into another room. After a while she came out with a hard, gloomy expression on her face. "Very well, Friedrich," she said, "let the lad go on his errand. Boy, why are you lying there in the cinders? Haven't you anything to do at home?"

The boy, with the mien of a fugitive, rose so hurriedly that all his limbs got tangled up and the "Holschen fiddle" nearly fell into the fire.

"Wait, Johannes," Friedrich said proudly, "I'll give you half of my bread and butter – it's too much for me... Mother always cuts a whole slice."

"Never mind," said Margret, "he's going home anyway."

"Yes, but he won't get anything. Uncle Simon eats at seven."

Margret turned to the boy. "Don't they keep anything for you? Who looks after you?"

"Nobody," the child stuttered.

"Nobody?" she repeated. "Here, take this – take it!" she added angrily. "You're called Niemand and nobody cares for you, God knows! And now go about your business! Friedrich, don't go with him, do you hear? Don't go through the village together."

"I only want to fetch wood from the shed," Friedrich answered.

When the two boys had gone, Margret threw herself onto a chair clapping her hands together, as an expression of deepest grief. Her face was as white as a sheet. "A false oath! A false oath!" she groaned. "Simon, Simon, how will you answer for it before God!"

Thus she sat for a time, unmoving, with compressed lips and in a state of complete abstraction. Friedrich was standing before her, and had already spoken to her twice before she replied. "What is it, what do you want?" she cried, starting up.

"I've brought you money," he said, more astonished than frightened.

"Money? Where?" She made a slight movement, and a small coin fell with a ring to the floor. Friedrich picked it up.

"Money from Uncle Simon, because I helped him with his work. I can earn something myself now."

"Money from Simon? Throw it away, throw it away! No, give it to the poor. But no, keep it," she whispered, scarcely audible, "we are poor ourselves. Who knows if we'll get along without begging!"

"I am to go back to Uncle on Monday and help him with the sowing."

"You go back to him? No, no, never!" She embraced her son passionately. "Never mind," she added, and the tears streamed suddenly down her sunken cheeks. "Go to him – he is my only brother, and there's a great deal of wicked gossip about these days! But keep God in your sight and don't forget your daily prayers!"

Margret laid her face against the wall and wept aloud. She had borne many a hard burden, ill treatment by her husband and, even worse, his death. It was a bitter moment when the widow had to relinquish to a creditor the last piece of her land and the plough stood idle before the house. But she had never felt as she did now. However, after she had wept for a whole evening and passed a whole night without sleep, she had come to the conclusion that her brother Simon could not be so godless after all – the boy certainly wasn't his, and likeness proved nothing. Had she not herself, forty years ago, lost a little sister who looked just like the foreign pedlar! What isn't one ready to believe when one has so little and is to lose even that through lack of faith!

From this time onwards Friedrich was seldom at home any longer. Simon seemed to have bestowed upon his nephew all the warmer feelings of which he was capable – at any rate, he missed him in his absence and continually sent messages when a domestic matter kept Friedrich with his mother for any length of time. Since then the boy had been quite changed: he had completely lost his dreamy ways, as his resolute step indicated; he began to pay attention to his appearance, and soon became known as a handsome and resourceful youth. His uncle, who could not live without his pet schemes, occasionally undertook quite important public works, for example road-building, in which Friedrich gained a reputation as one of his best workers and was regarded by everyone as his right-hand man – for although his physical strength had not yet reached maturity, there were few who had as much endurance. Till then Margret had only loved her son – now she began to be proud of him and even to feel a kind of respect for him as she saw him growing up quite independent of her help or even her counsel. Like most people, she considered the latter to be priceless, and therefore could not value highly enough his ability to dispense with such inestimable support.

Before turning eighteen, Friedrich had already secured a notable reputation among the young people of the village after winning a bet, which consisted in carrying a boar slain in the hunt on his back for over nine miles without resting. Sharing his glory, however, was just about the only advantage which Margret gained from this state of affairs, for Friedrich became ever more interested in his appearance and found it more and more difficult to pocket his pride whenever a lack of funds forced him to play second fiddle to anyone else in the village. Moreover, all his powers were directed to earning money outside the house; at home, in absolute contrast to his usual reputation, all regular work was irksome to him, and he preferred to submit to short periods of hard labour which soon permitted him to resume his former occupation as herdsman. This had already become unsuited to his age and exposed him to occasional ridicule – which he, however, soon silenced by a few hearty blows from his fist. Thus people grew used to seeing him sometimes the acknowledged dandy of the village, dressed up and in a happy mood at the head of the young people, sometimes a ragged herdsman stealing along behind the cows or, a lonely dreamer, lying apparently absent-minded in a forest clearing and plucking the moss from the trees.

About this time the slumbering laws were given a somewhat rude jolt by a band of timber thieves which, under the name of the "Blue Smocks", so far surpassed all their predecessors in cunning and impudence that it became intolerable even to the most forbearing of men. In direct contrast to the usual state of affairs, when the leaders of the pack can be pointed out, it had not been possible on this occasion, in spite of every vigilance, to name even a single individual. They received their name from their identically uniform dress, which made it difficult for them to be recognized if a forester should see a few isolated stragglers disappearing into a thicket. They laid waste the countryside like a swarm of pine looper caterpillars: whole areas of the forest were felled in a night and moved away at once, so that next morning nothing was found except chips of wood and tangled piles of unwanted top branches. The fact that cart tracks never led to a village, but always from the river and back again, proved that the thieves acted under the protection of – and perhaps with the help of – the ship owners. There must have been remarkably clever spies in the band: the foresters could stay awake at night for weeks on end without discovering anything, but, on the first night that they gave up their watch from sheer fatigue, no matter whether it was stormy or clear and moonlit, the destruction started again. It was strange that the people of the country around seemed as ignorant and nervous of the Blue Smocks' activities as the foresters themselves. Some villages declared positively that they did not belong to the Blue Smocks, but then no village could be strongly suspected, since B***, the most doubtful of all, had proved its innocence. Chance had brought this about: a wedding at which almost all the inhabitants of this village had been conspicuously present during the night, while at just this time the Blue Smocks had carried out one of their biggest expeditions.

The damage caused in the forests was, however, becoming intolerable, and therefore the measures against this evil were tightened up to an almost unprecedented degree. Patrols went out day and night, farm workers and servants were armed and drafted to foresters' groups. Nevertheless, success was only small, and the guards had scarcely left one end of the forest when the Blue Smocks entered from the other side. This lasted more than a year – guards and Blue Smocks, Blue Smocks and guards, always changing places like the sun and the moon, taking possession of the territory and never meeting.

It was three in the morning in July 1756. The moon shone in a clear sky, but its light began to wane, and in the east there already appeared a narrow yellow strip which lined the horizon and sealed the entrance to a narrow valley ravine as though with a golden ribbon. Friedrich lay in the grass, as was his custom, and whittled a willow rod, to whose gnarled end he tried to give a crude animal-like shape. He looked overtired, yawned, at times rested his head on a weather-beaten trunk and let his gaze, mistier than the horizon, roam over the entrance to the glen, which was almost overgrown with brushwood and young trees. His eyes lit up once or twice, and then assumed the glass-like glitter peculiar to them, but immediately afterwards he half-shut them again and yawned and stretched himself, as only lazy herdsmen may do. His dog lay some distance away close to the cows, which, unconcerned about the forest laws, nibbled at the young tender treetops as often as the grass, and blew into the fresh morning air. From the forest a dull crash was sometimes to be heard; the sound, accompanied by a long echo from the mountain slopes, lasted only a few seconds, and was repeated about every five to eight minutes. Friedrich paid no heed to it: only occasionally, when the noise was unusually loud and prolonged, he raised his head and let his gaze slowly glide over the different paths which ended at the bottom of the valley.

Already daybreak was fast approaching – the birds were beginning to twitter softly, and one could feel the dew rising from the earth. Friedrich had lowered himself down the trunk, and, hands clasped over his head, was gazing at the gently spreading flush of dawn. Suddenly he started – his expression changed abruptly, and, bending forwards, he listened for a moment like a hound scenting the trail. Then he quickly put two fingers to his mouth and gave a shrill, prolonged whistle. "Fidel, you wretched beast!" A hurtled stone struck the flanks of the unsuspecting animal, which, roused from sleep, first snapped in all directions and then ran howling on three legs to seek consolation at the very source of its discomfiture.

At that instant, the branches in a nearby thicket were thrust apart almost noiselessly to reveal a man dressed in a green hunting jacket with a silver coat of arms on the sleeve and holding a loaded shotgun. His gaze, roaming swiftly over the glen, came to rest with peculiar keenness on the youth; then he came forward, making signs in the direction of the thicket, and gradually seven or eight men came into view, all in similar clothing, hunting knives at their belts and cocked firearms in their hands.

"What was that, Friedrich?" asked the man who had first appeared.

"I wish this damned cur would fall dead here and now. He wouldn't mind if the cows nibbled the ears off my head."

"The swine saw us," another man said.

"Tomorrow I'll send you somewhere with a stone round your neck," Friedrich continued, and kicked at the dog.

"Don't play the fool, Friedrich! You know me and get my meaning!" These words were accompanied by a look which had a rapid effect.

"Think of my mother, sir!"

"I do. Didn't you hear anything in the forest?"

"In the forest?" The youth shot a swift glance at the forester's face. "Only your woodcutters."

"My woodcutters!"

The complexion of the forester, normally dusky, now changed to a deep purple. "How many of them are there, and where are they at work?"

"I don't know, sir – wherever you've sent them."

Brandis turned to his companions. "You go ahead, I'll be coming presently."

When, one after the other, they had disappeared into the thicket, Brandis came up close to the youth.

"Friedrich," he said, struggling to master his fury, "my patience is at an end. I feel like whipping you like a dog – and that's what you deserve! You, riff-raff without a penny to call your own! Soon you'll have to go begging, thank God, and that old witch, your mother, won't get even a mouldy crust at my door. But before that I'll have you both in jail."

With a convulsive movement Friedrich reached for a branch. He was as pale as death, and his eyes seemed to start from his head like crystal balls. But only for a moment. Then he assumed once more an expression of deep calm which almost suggested complete exhaustion.

"Sir," he said firmly, almost gently, "you've said things you can't answer for – and so have I, maybe. We'll call it quits, and now I'll tell you what you want to know. If you yourself didn't arrange for woodcutters to be there, it must be the Blue Smocks, for no cart came from the village. I can see the road, and there were four carts. I didn't see them, but heard them going up the glen." He faltered for a moment. "Could you really say that I have ever felled a tree in your district? Or that I have ever cut wood anywhere except when ordered? Just think whether you can say that."

An embarrassed mutter was the only answer from the forester, who, like most blunt men, was quick to repent his hot temper. He turned round irritably and walked towards the bushes.

"No, sir," Friedrich shouted, "if you want to join the other foresters, they have gone up past the beech."

"By the beech?" said Brandis doubtfully. "No, they went that way, to the Maste gorge."

"I tell you, past the beech – Big Henry's gun sling got caught on the crooked branch there. I saw it!"

The forester set out on the path indicated. All this time Friedrich had not left his place. Half lying with his arm round a dead branch, he looked steadily after the forester as he stalked down the partly overgrown footpath with the long cautious stride peculiar to his calling, as noiselessly as a fox climbs into a chicken roost. Here one branch sank behind him, there another – the outlines of his figure became ever more blurred. There was one last glint among the foliage – a steel button on his hunting jacket – and he was gone. While the forester was gradually disappearing, Friedrich's face lost its cold expression and finally mirrored his anxiety. Did he perhaps regret that he had not asked the forester to keep quiet about what he had said? He took a few steps towards the path, but soon stopped. "It's too late," he said to himself, and reached for his hat. The sound of light strokes came from the bushes, not twenty paces away. It was the forester, sharpening his gun flint. Friedrich listened. "No!" he then said resolutely. He collected his belongings and hastily drove the cattle along the glen.

About midday Margret was sitting by the hearth making tea. Friedrich had come home ill, complaining of a violent headache, and, in reply to her worried enquiry, had told her how the forester had angered him – in short, the whole incident just described with the exception of some minor details which he thought it best to keep to himself. Margret gazed silently and dejectedly into the boiling water. She was accustomed to hearing her son complain now and then, but today he seemed worn out as never before. Was he about to fall ill? She sighed deeply and dropped a block of wood which she had just picked up.

"Mother!" called Friedrich from the bedroom.

"What do you want?"

"Was that a shot?"

"No, I don't know what you mean."

"Perhaps it's only the throbbing in my head," he replied.

The woman from next door came in, and in a soft whisper retailed some trivial gossip, to which Margret listened without interest. Then she left.

"Mother!" called Friedrich.

Margret went to him.

"What did Frau Hülsmeyer say?"

"Oh, nothing, some rubbish or other!"

Friedrich sat up in bed.

"About Gretchen Siemers – you know, the old story... and there's not a grain of truth in it."

Friedrich lay down again. "I'll try to sleep," he said.

Margret sat by the hearth. She was spinning, and had thoughts which were far from pleasant. In the village the clock struck half-past eleven; the latch of the door was lifted, and Kapp, the clerk of the court, came in.

"Good day, Frau Mergel," he said. "Could you give me a drink of milk? I've just come from M***."

When Frau Mergel brought what he wanted, he asked, "Where's Friedrich?"

She was busy fetching a plate and didn't hear the question. He drank hesitantly and with short pauses. "Do you know," he then said, "the Blue Smocks last night again swept a whole piece of Maste Wood as bare as my hand."

"Goodness gracious!" she replied indifferently.

"The scoundrels ruin everything," the clerk went on. "If only they'd spare the young wood… But to cut oak saplings no thicker than my arm, not big enough for oars even! It's as though they liked doing harm to others as much as making a profit!"

"It's a shame!" Margret said.

The clerk had finished his drink, but still did not go. He seemed to have something on his mind. "Haven't you heard about Brandis?" he suddenly asked.

"No, he never comes here."

"You don't know then what has happened to him?"

"What happened?" Margret asked in suspense.

"He's dead!"

"Dead!" she cried. "Dead? Good Heavens! This very morning he went past here – he was in perfect health, with his gun on his back!"

"He's dead," the clerk repeated, watching her closely, "killed by the Blue Smocks. The corpse was brought into the village a quarter of an hour ago."

Margret clapped her hands in horror. "God above, don't judge him. He didn't know what he was doing!"

"Him!" cried the clerk. "The wretched murderer, you mean?"

From the bedroom deep groans were heard. Margret hurried in, and the clerk followed her. Friedrich was sitting up in bed, his face buried in his hands, moaning like a dying man.

"Friedrich, what's the matter?" said his mother.

"What's the matter?" the clerk repeated.

"Oh, my stomach, my head," he wailed.

"What's wrong with him?"

"God only knows," she replied. "He came home with the cows at about four o'clock because he felt so unwell."

"Friedrich, Friedrich, tell me, shall I go for the doctor?"

"No, no," he groaned, "it's only colic, and I'll soon get over it."

He lay back, his face twitching convulsively with pain, then his colour returned. "Go," he said feebly. "I must sleep... it'll pass."

"Frau Mergel," the clerk said earnestly, "are you sure that Friedrich came home at four and didn't go out again?"

She stared at him. "Ask any child in the street. Go out again... Would to God he could!"

"Has he said nothing to you about Brandis?"

"Yes, to tell the truth he said that Brandis abused him in the forest and jeered at our poverty, the scoundrel! But God forgive me, he's dead! Go away," she continued vehemently. "Did you come to insult honest people? Go!" She turned back to her son, and the clerk left.

"Friedrich, what's the matter?" his mother said. "You heard, I suppose. It's terrible, terrible – he died without confession and absolution!"

"Mother, Mother, for God's sake let me sleep. I can't stand any more of this!"

At this moment Johannes Niemand entered the room, long and thin as a hop pole, but ragged and shy as he had been five years before. His face was even paler than usual.

"Friedrich," he stuttered, "you are to come to your uncle straight away. He has work for you... but straight away."

Friedrich turned towards the wall. "I'm not coming," he said roughly. "I'm ill."

"But you must come!" Johannes panted. "He said I must bring you back."

Friedrich burst into a scornful laugh. "I'd like to see that!"

"Let him be... he can't," sighed Margret. "You can see how it is."

She went out for a few minutes. When she came back, Friedrich was already dressed.

"What are you thinking of?" she cried. "You can't – you shan't go!"

"What must be must be," he replied, already going out through the door with Johannes.

"Oh, God," sighed his mother. "When children are small, they trample on our laps – when they are big, on our hearts!"

The inquest had begun. That a crime had been committed was obvious – however, the evidence incriminating any actual person was so weak that, although all known facts cast the deepest suspicion on the Blue Smocks, only conjectures could be advanced. One clue seemed to throw some light on the case, but for various reasons it was scarcely heeded. The absence of the squire had obliged the clerk to begin the proceedings himself. He was sitting at the table; the room was crammed with peasants, some who had come from curiosity, some who, it was hoped, in the absence of actual witnesses, would provide information. Herdsmen who had been on watch that night, farm labourers who worked on the fields in the vicinity, all stood solidly and sturdily, their hands in their pockets, as though giving a silent demonstration that they were not prepared to have anything to do with the affair. Eight foresters were questioned: their statements tallied exactly. On the evening of the tenth, Brandis had ordered them out as guards, for he must have got wind of the Blue Smocks' plans, but he only spoke about this in a vague way. They had gone out at two o'clock in the morning and come across many signs of destruction which had put the head forester in a bad temper, otherwise everything had been quiet. Towards four o'clock Brandis had said: "They're making fools of us, let's go home." When they had turned the corner of Breme Mountain and the wind had changed direction at the same time, the felling of trees in Maste Wood was heard distinctly, and it was concluded from the quick sequence of the strokes that the Blue Smocks were at work. Now they had taken counsel for a while as to whether it would be feasible to attack the daring band with so much smaller numbers – and then, without coming to a definite decision, they had moved slowly towards the noise. Next followed the scene with Friedrich. After Brandis had sent them on without instructions, they had proceeded for a little while, and then, when they noticed that the noise, still some distance away, had ceased altogether, they halted to wait for the head forester. The delay had annoyed them, and after about ten minutes they had gone on until they reached the scene of destruction. All was over now: no further sound could be heard in the forest. Of twenty felled trunks, eight were still there, the others having already been taken away. It was inexplicable to them how this had been done, as no cart tracks were to be seen. At the same time, the dryness of the season and the fact that the ground was strewn with pine needles prevented footmarks from being detected, although the soil around looked as though it had been stamped firm. As it was now considered useless to await the head forester, they went quickly to the other end of the forest, in the hope that they might catch a glimpse of the thieves. Here, on leaving the woods, the cord on one forester's bottle had caught in the brambles, and, on looking round, he saw something glinting in the undergrowth. It was the belt buckle of the head forester, who was found lying behind the brambles, stretched out rigid, his right hand clutching his gun barrel, the other clenched and his forehead split open by an axe.

This was the statement of the foresters. Now it was the turn of the peasants, from whom, however, no information was to be obtained. Many said they had been still at home or busy elsewhere at about four o'clock, and one and all claimed to have seen nothing. What was to be done? They were all people of good repute living in the district, and their inconclusive testimony had to be accepted.

Friedrich was called in. He behaved in a manner no different from what was usual in him, showing neither nervousness nor impudence. The examination lasted quite a long time, and the questions were sometimes phrased rather slyly. However, he answered them all openly and positively, describing the scene between the forester and himself fairly truthfully, except for the end, which he considered it wiser not to mention. His alibi at the time of the murder was easily proved. The forester's body was lying on the edge of Maste Wood, over three quarters of an hour's walk away from the ravine in which he had spoken to Friedrich at about four o'clock, and from which Friedrich had driven his herd into the village only ten minutes later. Everyone had seen this – all the peasants present were eager to testify to it. He had spoken to one and nodded in greeting to another.

The clerk sat in his place, ill-humoured and embarrassed. Suddenly he reached behind him and placed something sparkling within Friedrich's vision. "Whose is this?"

Friedrich jumped back several paces. "Good Lord! I thought you meant to smash my skull in." His eyes had quickly alighted on the deadly instrument, and seemed fixed momentarily on a spot where a splinter had been broken off from the handle. "I don't know," he said firmly. It was the axe which had been found wedged in the skull of the head forester.

"Look at it carefully," continued the clerk of the court.

Friedrich took it in his hand, looked at it, at both top and bottom, and turned it over. Laying it indifferently on the table, he then said, "It is an axe like any other." A blood stain was visible. He seemed to shudder, but he repeated once more in a determined tone: "I don't recognize it."

The clerk sighed with vexation, for he didn't know how to proceed and had only tried that ruse in the hope of discovering the murderer by surprise tactics. There was nothing for it but to end the inquiry.

For the sake of those readers who are perhaps eager to learn the outcome of this affair, I must mention that it was never cleared up, although much was done to that end and several other official inquiries succeeded this one. The Blue Smocks seemed to have lost their courage through the stir that the incident caused and the stringent measures which followed. It was as though they had disappeared completely from this time forth, and although later many wood stealers were caught, no reason was ever found for connecting any of them with the notorious band. For twenty years afterwards the axe lay as a useless piece of evidence in the legal archives, where it is probably still to be found, complete with rust marks. It would be unfair to leave the reader's curiosity unsatisfied in a tale of fiction, but all this really happened – I cannot subtract or add anything.

Next Sunday Friedrich got up very early to go to confession. It was the Feast of the Assumption,* and the priests were already at their confessionals before dawn. After having dressed in the dark, Friedrich left the small closet furnished for him in Simon's house as noiselessly as possible. His prayer book, he thought, must be lying on the window sill in the kitchen, and he hoped to find it with the help of the feeble light from the moon. It was not there. In his search he cast his eyes all around, and suddenly started. Simon was standing at the door, almost unclothed – his gaunt form, unkempt, tangled hair and the pallor of his face caused by the moonlight made him seem weirdly changed. "Is he sleepwalking, maybe?" Friedrich thought, and remained quite still.

"Friedrich, where are you going?" whispered the old man.

"Oh, it's you, uncle? I'm going to confession."

"That's what I thought. Go in God's name, but confess like a good Christian."

"So I will," said Friedrich.

"Remember the Ten Commandments. Thou shalt not bear witness against thy neighbour."

"False witness!"

"No, none at all: you've got it wrong. Anyone who denounces somebody else in confession is unworthy to receive the sacrament."

Both remained silent. "Uncle, how do you come to speak of that?" Friedrich then said. "Your conscience is not clear – you have lied to me."

"I? What?"

"Where is your axe?"

"My axe? On the threshing floor."

"Did you give it a new handle? Where is the old one?"

"You'll find it in the woodshed this morning. Go," he continued, "I thought you were a man, but you're just an old woman who thinks the house is on fire when her stove is smoking. "Look," he went on, "on my hope of salvation, I don't know any more of the affair than that doorpost. I was long home by then," he added.

Friedrich stood there dubious and uneasy. He would have given much to have been able to see his uncle's face. But while they had been whispering, the sky had clouded over.

"I am guilty of a great sin," Friedrich sighed, "in having sent him the wrong way... although... But I never thought of that, really not. Uncle, I have you to thank for a guilty conscience."

"Go on then, confess!" Simon whispered, his voice shaking. "Dishonour the sacrament by tale-bearing and put a spy on the track of poor wretches. If he doesn't talk straight away, he will soon find ways of snatching crusts of bread from their very mouths... Go!"

Friedrich stood irresolute. He heard a slight sound. The clouds passed over; the moonlight again fell on the door: it was closed. Friedrich did not go to confession that morning.

Unfortunately the impression which this incident made on Friedrich died away all too quickly. Who can doubt that Simon did all he could to lead his adopted son along the paths that he took himself? And in Friedrich were characteristics which made this all too easy: frivolity, a fiery temper and, above all, a boundless arrogance. Thus he did not always scorn mere outward pretence, and then moved heaven and earth to escape possible shame by providing a foundation for his claims. His nature was not ignoble, but he accustomed himself to preferring inner to outer shame. One can only say that he got used to making a show, while his mother lived in want.

This unhappy change in his character developed, however, over several years, during which it was noticed that Margret spoke less and less of her son, gradually sinking into a state of neglect such as would never have been considered possible before. She became timid, dilatory, even untidy, and many thought that she was no longer right in the head. Friedrich became even louder in consequence; he never missed a fair or a wedding, and, since his extremely touchy sense of honour did not allow him to ignore silent disapproval from others, he appeared to be always on the defensive – not so much to defy public opinion as to guide it along a path which suited him. In outer appearance he was neat, sober, apparently candid, but actually he was cunning, boastful and often brutal – a man who gave pleasure to nobody, least of all to his mother, and who nevertheless had acquired through his dreaded boldness and still more dreaded malice a certain power in the village, as people came to realize that they could neither really fathom him nor foresee how he might turn out in the end. Only one lad in the village, Wilm Hülsmeyer, conscious of his power and easy circumstances, dared to oppose him – and since he could use words with greater skill than Friedrich and always knew how to make a joke out of it when a thrust went home, he was the only person whom Friedrich tried to avoid.

Four years went by. It was October, and the mild autumn of 1760, which filled all the barns with corn and all the cellars with wine, had also covered this corner of the earth with its riches, and one saw more drunken men, heard of more brawls and stupid pranks than ever. Merrymaking went on everywhere – a "long weekend" came into fashion, and, as soon as anybody had a few shillings to spare, he wanted to have a wife as well who would help him to eat today and starve tomorrow.

Now there took place in the village a fine, respectable wedding at which the guests could expect more than a badly tuned fiddle, a glass of brandy and the high spirits which they brought with them. Everybody had been up since an early hour; clothes were aired in front of every door, and the village had looked like an old-clothes shop all day long. Since many people from other parts were expected, all the inhabitants wanted to uphold the honour of their village. It was seven in the evening, and the celebrations were in full swing – shouts of merriment and laughter everywhere, the low-ceilinged rooms crammed to suffocation with figures in blue, red and yellow, like cattle pens into which too large a herd has been huddled. On the threshing floor there was dancing – that is, whoever had captured two feet of space for himself whirled around on it and tried by shrieking to make up for lack of movement. The orchestra was brilliant: the first fiddle excelling as a recognized virtuoso, the second and a double bass with three strings played ad lib by amateurs. There was brandy and coffee in abundance; all the guests were dripping with sweat – in short, it was a memorable occasion.

Friedrich swaggered around like a peacock in his new sky-blue coat and staked his claim as the local dandy. When the squire and his family also arrived, he was sitting bolt upright behind the double bass, playing on the lowest string with great vigour and much dignity. "Johannes!" he shouted imperiously, and his protégé came forwards from the dance floor, where he too had tried to fling about his clumsy legs and to whoop. Friedrich handed him the bow, and, indicating his desire by a proud movement of his head, he joined the dancers. "Now, you fiddlers, play the 'Monk of Istrup'!" The favourite dance was played, and Friedrich made such leaps, in full view of his master, that the cows close by drew in their horns, lowing loudly and rattling their chains. High above the others, Friedrich's fair head shot up and down like a pike turning somersaults in the water. From every corner there came the shrieking of girls, to whom he, as he tossed his head, paid homage by flicking his long flaxen hair in their faces.

"That will do now!" he said at last, and, dripping with sweat, went over to the refreshment table. "Long live our gracious lord and lady and all the high-born princes and princesses, and if anyone won't drink to them, I'll smack his ears till he hears the angels singing!" A loud cheer greeted the gallant toast, and Friedrich made his bow. "Don't take offence, lord and lady, for we are only simple peasants!" At this moment there arose a tumult at the other end of the threshing floor – shouts, scolding, laughter, all mingling in confusion. "Butter thief, butter thief!" cried a few of the children, and somebody made his way, or rather was pushed, through the crowd – Johannes Niemand, cowering and struggling for all he was worth to reach the exit.

"What is it? What's Johannes done?" shouted Friedrich imperiously.

"You'll see that soon enough," panted an old woman, holding an apron and a dishcloth. What a disgrace! Johannes, poor devil, who had to be content with the very worst at home, had tried to help himself to half a pound of butter to provide for hard times to come. Forgetting that he had hidden it in his pocket after having wrapped it neatly in his handkerchief, he had stood in front of the kitchen fire, and now he was put to shame by the fat running down his coat tails. There was a general uproar – the girls jumped away, for fear of soiling their dresses, or pushed the offender forwards. Others made room for him, from pity as well as foresight. Friedrich, however, moved towards him: "You miserable hound!" he cried. He slapped his patient protégé hard in the face several times, pushed him towards the door and gave him a good kick from behind to help him on his way.

He returned crestfallen: his dignity had been injured; the laughter he heard on all sides cut him to the quick – and although he tried to get back into his stride with a valiant whoop, it did not work any longer. He was about to take refuge again behind the double bass, but first he sought to create a sensation by taking out his silver pocket watch, at that time a rare and costly adornment. "It's nearly ten," he said. "Now for the bridal minuet! I'll play for it."

"A fine-looking watch!" said the swineherd, thrusting his face forwards in respectful curiosity.

"What did it cost?" asked Wilm Hülsmeyer, Friedrich's rival.

"Do you want to pay for it?" asked Friedrich.

"Have *you* paid for it?" Wilm answered.

Friedrich gave him a proud look and reached in silent majesty for the fiddle bow.

"Well," said Hülsmeyer, "it's happened before. You know very well Franz Ebel had a fine watch too, before Aaron the Jew took it off him again."

Friedrich did not answer, but signed proudly to the first violin, and they began to play with all their might.

In the mean time, the squire and his family had entered the room where women from the neighbourhood had placed the headband round the bride's forehead as a symbol of her married state. The young girl wept a good deal, partly because the custom required it, partly from genuine anxiety. She was to take charge of a disorderly household under the supervision of an ill-humoured old man, whom she was supposed to love into the bargain. He stood beside her, quite unlike the bridegroom of the Song of Solomon, who stepped into the room like a "tabernacle for the sun".* "You've cried enough now," he said crossly. "Remember that I'm making you happy, not you me!"

She looked humbly up at him and vaguely felt that he was right. The ceremony was at an end; the young bride had drunk her husband's health; young wags had followed the old custom of looking through the tripod to see if her headband was straight, and they all jostled their way back to the threshing floor, from which noise and ceaseless peals of laughter could be heard. Friedrich was no longer there. He had been thoroughly, even intolerably discredited when Aaron the Jew, a butcher and occasional second-hand dealer from the town nearby, had suddenly appeared and, after a short unsatisfactory exchange of words, had loudly pressed him, in the presence of all the guests, to pay thirty shillings for a watch already delivered to him on the previous Easter. Friedrich had gone away seeming utterly crushed, followed by the Jew, who kept on shouting: "Alas! Why didn't I listen to sensible people? Didn't they tell me a hundred times that you wore all you had on your back and hadn't a crust of bread in the larder?" The threshing floor rocked with laughter; many guests had pushed their way out into the yard in pursuit. "Get hold of the Jew! He'll outweigh a pig, you'll see!" some shouted, while others had grown serious. "Friedrich looked as white as a sheet," said an old woman, and the crowd parted as the squire's carriage turned into the yard.

Herr von S*** was in an ill humour on the way home, as invariably happened when his wish to maintain his popularity made him attend such festivities. He was gazing silently out of the carriage. "What are those two figures?" he indicated two shadow-like forms running like ostriches in front of the carriage. Now they slipped into the manor house. "So we have the ghosts of a couple of pigs from our own sty as well!" sighed Herr von S***. Having arrived home, he found the large hall filled with all the servants surrounding two farmhands, who had collapsed pale and breathless on the stairs. They said they had been pursued by the spirit of old Mergel when they were returning home through Brede Wood. At first there had been a rustling and crackling on the heights above them; after that a rattling high up in the air like two sticks struck together; then suddenly a shriek and the words, heard quite distinctly, "Have mercy on my poor soul!" coming down from far above. One claimed to have also seen glittering eyes sparkling through the branches, and both had run as fast as their legs would carry them.

"Rubbish!" said the squire irritably, and went to his room to change his clothes. Next morning the fountain in the garden would not work, and it was found that somebody had moved a pipe, apparently to look for the head of a horse which had been buried there many years before – this was reckoned to be a guaranteed protection against witches and apparitions.

"Hm," said the squire. "What the rascals don't steal, the fools spoil."

Three days later, a fearful storm was raging. It was midnight, but everyone at the manor house was up. The squire was standing at the window, looking anxiously into the darkness, across his fields. The leaves and branches were flying past the window panes; sometimes a tile came down and smashed on the paved courtyard.

"Terrible weather!" said Herr von S***.

His wife looked frightened. "Has somebody really seen to the fire?" she said. "Gretchen, have another look at it, it's best to put it out altogether. Come, let us say the Gospel of St John as a prayer."

All knelt down, and the lady of the house began: "In the beginning was the Word, and the Word was with God, and the Word was God."* A fearful clap of thunder sounded. Everyone shrank – then there was a terrible screaming and tumult drawing ever nearer. "What, in God's name? Is the house on fire?" cried Frau von S***, and buried her face in a chair. The door was flung open, and the wife of Aaron the Jew rushed in, pale as death, her hair windswept about her head, dripping with rain. She threw herself on her knees before the squire. "Justice!" she cried. "Justice! My husband has been killed!" And she collapsed unconscious.

It was only too true, and the investigation which followed proved that Aaron the Jew had died from a single blow on the temple with a blunt instrument, probably a stick. On the left temple was a bruise, but no other injury.

The statements of the Jew's wife and her servant Samuel ran as follows. Three days before, Aaron had gone out in the afternoon in order to buy cattle, and had said at the time that he would probably be away overnight, as some long outstanding debts in B*** and S*** had to be collected. He said that he would stay the night in B*** with the butcher Salomon. When he had not returned home on the following day, his wife had become very anxious, and had finally set out to look for him on that day at three o'clock in the afternoon, accompanied by her servant and the big butcher's dog. At Salomon's nobody knew where Aaron was: he had not been there at all. Then they had gone to all the peasants with whom they knew Aaron had contemplated business deals. Only two had seen him, and these actually on the same day on which he had left. Meanwhile, it had grown very late. The woman's apprehension drove her home, for she nourished a faint hope of meeting him there. And so they had been overtaken in Brede Wood by the thunderstorm, and had sought shelter under a large beech tree standing on the mountain side. While they were there, the dog had been sniffing about in a strange way which attracted their attention, and finally, ignoring all calls, had run away in the forest. Then suddenly, during a flash of lightning, the woman saw something white beside her on the moss. It was her husband's stick. Almost at the same moment, the dog broke through a thicket, carrying something in its mouth – her husband's shoe. Soon they found the corpse of the Jew in a ditch filled with dead leaves. This was the statement by the servant, supported only in a general way by the wife's evidence; her excessive excitement had abated, and she now seemed half bewildered, or rather in a stupor. "An eye for an eye, a tooth for a tooth!"* These were the only words that she sometimes muttered.

That same night the police were summoned to arrest Friedrich. A warrant was not required, for Herr von S*** himself had witnessed a scene which inevitably threw the strongest suspicion on him. In addition, there was the ghost story of that evening, the knocking together of sticks in Brede Wood, the cry from above. Since the clerk was absent just then, Herr von S*** directed the proceedings, and indeed with greater speed than would otherwise have been the case. However, dawn had already begun to break before the police had surrounded, as quietly as possible, poor Margret's home. The squire himself knocked at the door, and scarcely a minute elapsed before it was opened and Margret appeared, fully dressed. Herr von S*** started back – because of her deathly pallor and stony expression, he almost failed to recognize her.

"Where is Friedrich?" he asked in an unsteady voice.

"Look for him," she said, and sat down on a chair.

The squire still hesitated for a moment. Then he said roughly, "Come in, come in! What are we waiting for?"

They entered Friedrich's room. He was not there, but his bed was still warm. They went up into the loft, down into the cellar, poked about in the straw, looked behind every barrel, even in the baking oven – he was not there. Some men went into the garden, looked behind the fence and up into the apple trees. He was not to be found.

"He's got clean away!" said the squire with very mixed feelings. The sight of the old woman had a powerful effect on him. "Hand over the key to that chest." Margret did not answer. "Hand over the key!" the squire repeated, and now he noticed for the first time that the key was in the lock. The contents of the chest were revealed: the good Sunday clothes of the fugitive and the shabby finery of his mother; then two shrouds with black ribbons, one for a man, the other for a woman. Herr von S*** was deeply moved. Right at the bottom of the trunk lay the silver watch and some documents in a very legible hand, one of them signed by a man strongly suspected of being connected with the timber thieves. Herr von S*** took them away to look through, and they left the house without Margret giving any further sign of life, except that she ceaselessly gnawed at her lips and blinked her eyes.

Arriving at the manor house, the squire found the clerk, who had already come home on the previous evening and now said he had slept through the whole affair, since His Lordship had not sent for him.

"You always come too late," said Herr von S*** irritably. "Wasn't there some old woman in the village who told your maid about it? And why didn't someone wake you then?"

"Your Lordship," replied Kapp, "it is true that my Anne Marie heard of the affair about an hour before I did, but she knew that you were conducting the proceedings yourself, and also," he added with a plaintive expression, "that I was so dog-tired!"

"A fine police force!" the squire muttered. "Every old hag in the village knows all about things which should be kept secret." Then he continued angrily: "He'd have to be a really stupid devil of a criminal to get caught!"

Both were silent for a while. "My driver had lost his way in the dark," the clerk began again. "We stopped for over an hour in the forest; there was a terrific storm, and I thought the wind would blow the carriage over. At last, when the rain grew less heavy, we set out again towards Zelle Field, hoping for the best, but without being able to see a hand's breadth in front of us. Then the driver said: 'If only we don't get too near to the stone quarries!' I was frightened myself – I told him to stop and struck a light in order, at least, to draw comfort from my pipe. Suddenly we heard, quite close to us, directly beneath us, the clock striking. Your Lordship will understand that I was frightened to death. I jumped out of the carriage, for one can trust one's own legs, but not those of a horse. And so I stood, in mud and rain, without moving, until, thank God, it soon began to get light. And where had we halted? Close to Heerse Valley, with the tower of Heerse church directly below us. If we had gone on twenty paces, we would both have been dead men."

"That was certainly no joke," replied the squire, somewhat mollified.

Meanwhile, he had looked through the papers he had taken away with him. There were letters, mostly from moneylenders demanding payment of sums borrowed. "I would never have thought," he murmured, "that the Mergels were so up to their necks in trouble."

"Yes, and that it should come to light in this way," replied Kapp, "will be no small annoyance for Frau Margret."

"Good gracious, she's not thinking of that now!" With these words the squire stood up and left the room in order to make the legal post-mortem examination with Kapp. The investigation was short, and it was established that death had been caused by violent means and that the probable culprit had fled. The evidence against him had been indeed incriminating, but not conclusive without personal confession, though his flight was certainly very suspicious. Thus the legal proceedings had to be brought to a close without a satisfactory outcome.

The Jews in the neighbourhood had shown great interest in the affair. The house of the widow was never empty of mourners and people offering advice and help. As long as one could remember, so many Jews had not been seen together in L***. Embittered by the murder of their fellow Jew, they had spared neither effort nor money to track down the criminal. It was even said that one of them, commonly known as "Joel the Shark", had promised one of his customers, who owed him several hundreds and whom he considered to be a particularly sly fellow, remission of the whole sum in return for his help in getting Mergel arrested – for it was generally believed among the Jews that the murderer could only have escaped with generous assistance and was probably still in the district. However, when all this was of no avail and the legal inquiry had been declared closed, there appeared on the following morning at the manor house a number of the most respected Israelites to make a business proposition to His Lordship. The object of this was the beech under which Aaron's staff had been found and where the murder had probably been committed. "Do you want to fell it, just as it is, in full leaf?" asked the squire.

"No, Your Lordship, it must stand in winter and summer alike, as long as a splinter of it remains."

"But whenever I have the forest felled, the beech will hinder the growth of the saplings."

"Yes, but we don't want it at the market price." They offered fifty pounds for it. The bargain was concluded, and all foresters given strict orders not to damage the Jew's beech in any way. Soon after about sixty Jews, led by their rabbi, were to be seen walking in procession to Brede Wood, all of them silent and with their eyes on the ground. They remained over an hour in the forest and then returned, in the same grave and solemn manner, passing through the village to Zelle Field, where they dispersed. Next morning these characters were to be seen carved on the beech with an axe:

אִם תַּעֲבוֹר בַּמָּקוֹם הַזֶּה יִכְּגַע בְּךָ פַּאֲשֶׁר אַתָּה עָשָׂה לִי

And where was Friedrich? Doubtless far away, far enough to be beyond the reach of the short arms of such an impotent police force. Out of sight, out of mind, he was soon forgotten. Uncle Simon seldom spoke of him, and then harshly. The Jew's widow finally took solace in another husband. Only poor Margret remained uncomforted.

About six months later, the squire was reading, in the presence of the clerk, some letters he had just received. "Strange, most peculiar!" he said. "Just think, Kapp, perhaps Mergel is innocent of the murder after all. The president of the court at P*** has just written to me: '*Le vrai n'est pas toujours vraisemblable**' – I often find that true in my profession, and had another example of it recently. Do you know that your faithful servant Friedrich Mergel is as unlikely to have killed the Jew as you or I? Unfortunately proof is lacking, but it is very probable that he did not. A member of the Schlemming gang (most of which, by the way, we now have under lock and key) named Rag-and-Bone Moses stated when last examined that he repented in particular his murder of a fellow Jew, Aaron. He had killed him in the forest, and yet only found sixpence on him. Unhappily the proceedings were interrupted, and while we were at table the dog of a Jew hanged himself with his garter. What do you make of it? It is true that Aaron is a common name, etc., etc.'"

"What do you make of it?" repeated the squire. "And why then did the dolt of a boy run away?"

The clerk reflected. "Well, perhaps because of timber thieving, which we were looking into just then. Isn't it often said: the wicked runs from his own shadow? Mergel's conscience was black enough, even without this stain."

With that they let the matter rest. Friedrich had gone, disappeared and – with him on the same day – Johannes Niemand, the wretched Johannes, whom nobody would miss.

Twenty-eight years had elapsed – a very long time, almost half a human lifespan. The squire had grown very old and grey; his good-tempered clerk Kapp had long been buried. Men, animals and plants had come to life, matured and passed away – only the manor house of B***, as grey and stately as ever, looked down on the cottages, which, like old consumptive people, seemed always on the point of collapsing and yet continued to stand. It was Christmas Eve, 1788. Snowdrifts to a depth of nearly twelve feet lay on the roads, and a penetrating frosty air covered the window panes in heated rooms with rime. Midnight was near, yet faint little lights glimmered everywhere from among the mounds of snow, and in each house the inhabitants knelt to await in prayer the coming of Christmas, as is, or was then at least, the custom in Catholic countries. Just then a figure was to be observed moving slowly down to the village from Brede Heights. The traveller seemed very exhausted or ill: he uttered deep groans, and dragged himself laboriously through the snow.

Halfway down the slope he stopped, leant on his crook and stared fixedly at the points of light. It was so quiet everywhere, so cold and dead, it made one think of will-o'-the-wisps in churchyards. Now the clock in the tower struck twelve. The last stroke rumbled and died away slowly – in the nearest house some people began to sing quietly, and the hymn, swelling from house to house, spread through the whole village:

This day is born an infant rare,
To us it hath befell,
Of virgin pure – the tidings fair
Rejoicing all men tell.
And had the childling been not born,
We all would sooth have been forlorn:
His birth is our salvation.
O Jesu, dearest Jesu, Lord
Once born as Man, by us adored,
Redeem us from damnation.

The man on the slope had sunk to his knees and with trembling voice was trying to join in the singing, but the result was only a loud sobbing, as his great, scalding tears fell on the snow. In a low voice he accompanied with a prayer the singing of the second verse, then the third and fourth verses too. The carol came to an end, and the lights in the houses were moved about, whereupon the man rose painfully to his feet and crept down to the village. Panting, he toiled on his way past several houses before stopping at one and knocking softly on the door.

"What's that, then?" said a woman from within. "The door rattles and yet the wind's not blowing."

He knocked harder. "For Heaven's sake, let in a poor, half-frozen creature returned from Turkish slavery!"

There was whispering in the kitchen.

"Go to the inn," answered another voice. "The fifth house from here!"

"For God's sake, let me in! I have no money."

After some hesitation, the door was opened, and a man shone the lamp outside. "Very well, come in," he said. "You won't cut our throats."

Besides the man there were also in the kitchen a middle-aged woman, her old mother and five children. They all crowded round the stranger as he entered and inspected him with shy curiosity. He was a wretched figure with a crooked neck, a bent back, his whole frame broken and feeble – long, snow-white hair hanging round a face disfigured by years of suffering. The woman went silently to the hearth and put a few more faggots on the fire. "We cannot give you a bed," she said, "but I'll make you a good shakedown here – you must manage as best you can."

"God bless you!" replied the stranger. "I am used to much worse."

The homecomer was recognized as Johannes Niemand, and he himself confirmed that he was the same person who had once fled with Friedrich Mergel.

The following day the village was full of the adventures of one who had been missing for so long. Everybody wanted to see the man from Turkey, and many seemed almost astonished that he still looked like other people. Of course the young ones could not remember him, but the old made out his features well enough, deplorably distorted as they were.

"Johannes, Johannes, how grey you've become!" said an old woman. "And where did you get your crooked neck?"

"From carrying wood and water as a slave," he replied.

"And what became of Mergel? You ran away together, didn't you?"

"Yes, we did, but I don't know where he is – we were parted. If you think of him, pray for him," he added. "He will certainly need your prayers."

He was asked why Friedrich ran away, since he didn't kill the Jew. "Didn't?" said Johannes, and listened intently to the story which the squire had spread conscientiously to wipe the stain from Mergel's name. "So it was all for nothing," he said thoughtfully. "So much endured, all for nothing!" He sighed deeply, and now it was his turn to ask many questions. Simon had died long ago, but not before he had become completely impoverished through lawsuits and debtors whom he could not sue because – so it was said – his business with them had been of a shady nature. He had finally eaten the bread of a beggar and died on a pile of straw in a shed which was not his own. Margret had lived longer, but in complete apathy. As she let everything given to her go to rack and ruin, the village people had soon tired of helping, for it is natural to man to abandon those who are actually the most helpless, those cases where assistance does not have a lasting effect but is constantly needed. Nevertheless, she had not suffered actual want: the squire's family took good care of her, sending her food every day and arranging for medical treatment when her ailing health had declined to complete emaciation. In her house there now lived the son of the former swineherd, who had so much admired Friedrich's watch on that unfortunate evening. "All gone, all dead!" sighed Johannes.

In the evening, when darkness had fallen and the moon was shining, he was seen hobbling about the churchyard in the snow. Although he did not go to any grave to offer a prayer, he seemed to stare at some of them from a distance; and that was how Brandis the forester found him. Brandis, the son of the murdered man, had been sent by the squire to fetch him to the manor house.

Entering the sitting room, he gazed around shyly, as though dazzled by the light. The baron was sitting in his armchair, much shrivelled by age but with the same bright eyes and little red cap on his head that he had twenty-eight years before. Beside him Johannes saw Her Ladyship, who had also grown old, very old.

"Now, Johannes," said the squire, "give us a proper account of your adventures. But really," he added, examining him through his spectacles, "you must have had a bad time of it in Turkey!"

Johannes began to relate how Mergel had called him away from the cattle he was minding that night and told him he must go with him.

"But why did the stupid boy run away then? You know that he was innocent?"

Johannes looked down in front of him. "I don't know exactly – I think it was something to do with timber thieving. Simon was mixed up in all kinds of deals. I wasn't told about them, but I don't think that things were as they should be."

"What did Friedrich say to you?"

"Nothing, except that we would have to run for it, as they were after us. So we ran as far as Heerse – it was still dark when we got there, and we hid behind the big cross in the churchyard until it became somewhat lighter, for we were afraid of falling into the stone quarries at Zelle Field. When we had sat there for a while, we suddenly heard snorting and stamping above us and saw long streaks of fire in the air just over Heerse church tower. We jumped up and ran as hard as we could straight ahead, hoping for the best, and as dawn broke, we were really on the right road to P***."

Johannes still seemed to shudder at the memory, and the squire thought of his dead clerk Kapp and his adventure on the slope above Heerse. "Strange!" he said with a laugh. "You were so close to one another... but go on."

Now Johannes related how they had gone through P*** and over the frontier without mishap. From there they had made their way as journeying apprentices to Freiburg in Breisgau. "I had my bread bag with me, and Friedrich a little bundle as well, so that people believed our story," he said.

In Freiburg they had taken service with the Austrians, who had not wanted Johannes, but Friedrich had insisted. And so he was sent to the baggage train. "We remained for the winter in Freiburg, and had quite an easy time – me too, because Friedrich often reminded me of things and helped me if I did anything wrong. In the spring we had to march to Hungary, and in the autumn the war with the Turks started. I can't tell you much about it, for I was captured in the first battle and have been since then in Turkish slavery for twenty-six years!"

"Good Heavens, that's terrible!" said Frau von S***.

"Bad enough, the Turks don't treat us Christians any better than dogs. The worst was that my strength gave way because of the hard work. Also, as I grew older, I was still expected to do as much as years before."

He was silent for a while. "Yes," he then said, "it was beyond human strength and patience. I too could not endure it. From there I came on board a Dutch ship."

"How did you get there?" asked the squire.

"They fished me out of the Bosporus," replied Johannes. The baron looked at him disapprovingly and then held up a warning finger, but Johannes went on with his story. He did not have a much better time of it on the ship. An epidemic of scurvy set in, and all those who were not desperately ill had to take on more than their usual work. The rope's end ruled as harshly as the Turkish whip. "Finally," he concluded, "when we came to Holland, to Amsterdam, I was released because I couldn't be used. The merchant who owned the ship took pity on me and wanted to make me his porter, but" – he shook his head – "I preferred to beg my way here."

"That was silly enough of you," said the squire.

Johannes sighed deeply. "Oh sir, I had to spend my life among Turks and heretics – may I not at least lie in a Catholic churchyard?"

The squire had taken out his purse. "There you are, Johannes. Go now and come back again soon. You must tell me more about it – today your story was somewhat confused. You're still very tired, aren't you?"

"Very tired," Johannes replied, pointing to his forehead, "and my thoughts are sometimes so queer, I can't rightly say why."

"I know," said the baron. "That started a long time ago. Now go! The Hülsmeyers will, I hope, keep you for the night. Come again tomorrow."

Herr von S*** had the deepest sympathy with the poor fellow, discussing with his family until the following day where Johannes might find lodgings. They decided that he was to eat daily at the manor house, and that ways and means of clothing him could be found.

"Sir," said Johannes, "I can still do something or other. I can make wooden spoons, and you can use me as a messenger."

Herr von S*** shook his head sympathetically. "That wouldn't work out very well."

"Oh yes it would, sir, once I get started – I can't go fast, but I get there, and it won't be as hard for me as one might think."

"Well," said the baron doubtfully, "do you want to try it? Here is a letter to go to P***. There is no particular hurry."

On the following day Johannes moved into his little room in the house of a widow in the village. He carved spoons, ate at the manor house and ran errands for His Lordship. On the whole he had a tolerable time of it: the squire and his family were very kind, and Herr von S*** often talked long with him about Turkey, service in the Austrian army and the sea.

"Johannes could tell much," he said to his wife, "if only he weren't such a downright simpleton."

"More melancholic than simple," she replied. "I'm always afraid he'll go really mad one day."

"Don't worry!" answered the baron. "He has been a simpleton all his life, and simple people never go mad."

After some time, Johannes was absent on an errand far longer than was expected. The warm-hearted wife of the squire was very concerned for him, and was already about to send out people to look for him when she heard him hobble up the stairs.

"You were away a long time, Johannes," she said. "I thought you had lost your way in Brede Wood."

"I went through Pine Valley."

"But that's a long way round – why didn't you go through Brede Wood?"

He looked up at her sadly. "People told me the wood had been felled, and that now there are so many cross paths, so I was afraid I wouldn't get out again. I'm getting old and silly," he added slowly.

"Did you see," said Frau von S*** to her husband afterwards, "how queer his eyes were? He didn't look us in the face. I tell you, Ernst, he'll come to a sad end."

Meanwhile, September drew near. The fields were bare, the leaves began to fall, and many a consumptive felt the shears of fate at his life thread. Johannes, too, seemed to suffer under the influence of the approaching equinox. Those who saw him in those days say he looked strangely agitated and talked incessantly to himself in a soft voice (he sometimes did this in any case, but not often). Finally he failed to come home one evening. It was thought that the squire or his wife had sent him on an errand, but he did not return on the second day either, and by the third his landlady was worried. She went to the manor house to make enquiries.

"No, indeed," said the squire, "I know nothing of his whereabouts, but call the gamekeeper and the forester's son Wilhelm quickly! If the poor cripple has fallen, even into a dry ditch, he won't be able to get out again," he added with feeling. "Who knows whether he hasn't broken one of his crooked legs. Take the hounds with you," he shouted to the gamekeepers as they moved off, "and, above all, look in the ditches – the quarries!" he shouted louder.

The gamekeepers returned home some hours later, having found no trace of Johannes. Herr von S*** was in a state of great alarm. "To think that he would just have to lie like a log and be unable to help himself! But he may be still alive – a man can hold out without food for three days." He set out himself. Enquiries were made at every house, horns were blown everywhere, men shouted, hounds were driven on to search – in vain! A child had seen him sitting at the edge of Brede Wood, whittling a spoon. "But he cut it right in two," said the little girl. That had been two days before. In the afternoon another clue was found. Again it was a child who noticed him on the other side of the wood, where he had been sitting in the bushes, his face on his knees, as though he were sleeping. That had been on the day before. It seemed that he had been wandering the whole time near Brede Wood.

"If only the damned bushes weren't so thick! Nobody can get through them," said the squire. The hounds were driven among the young trees; there was blowing of horns and hallooing, but eventually they all returned home out of spirits, after having made sure that the animals had combed through the whole wood.

"Don't give up! Don't give up!" begged Frau von S***. "Better a few steps for nothing than that something should be overlooked."

The baron was almost as worried as she was. His alarm even drove him to visit Johannes's room, although he was certain of not finding him there. He had his room unlocked. His bed stood still unmade, as he had left it; his good coat, which Her Ladyship had had made for him out of the old hunting jacket of her husband, was hanging nearby; on the table lay a bowl, six new wooden spoons and a box. The squire opened it. Five pennies lay in it, wrapped neatly in paper, and four silver waistcoat buttons, which the squire looked at with interest. "A souvenir from Mergel," he murmured, and went out, for he felt oppressed in the close atmosphere of the tiny closet. The investigations were continued till there was no doubt that Johannes was no longer in the district – not alive, at least. So he had disappeared a second time. Would he be found again? Perhaps only after many years his bones would be discovered in a dry ditch? There was little hope of seeing him again alive – certainly not if he were absent for another twenty-eight years.

A fortnight later young Brandis was returning home one morning from an inspection of his district, and his path took him through Brede Wood. It was an unusually warm day for the time of year. The air seemed to quiver, not a bird was singing – only the ravens croaked wearily from the branches and turned their gaping beaks towards the air. Brandis was very tired. Sometimes he took off his cap, well heated by the sun, sometimes he put it on again. It was all equally unbearable, and pushing one's way through the young trees, which grew knee-high, was very laborious. All around there was no tree except the Jew's beech. He made for it as quickly as he could and dropped under it, dead tired, onto the shady moss. The coolness penetrated his limbs so pleasantly that he closed his eyes. "Disgusting toadstools!" he muttered, half asleep. For there is in that district a type of very succulent toadstool which only grows for a few days and then collapses in decay emitting an intolerable smell. Brandis thought that he could smell such unpleasant neighbours. He turned from side to side once or twice, but could not bring himself to get up. Meanwhile, his dog was jumping about, scratching at the trunk of the tree and barking upwards. "What is it then, Bello, a cat?" Brandis murmured. He half-opened his eyelids, and the Jewish inscription, very much deformed by bark growth, but still quite legible, caught his attention. He shut his eyes again. The dog went on barking and finally put its cold nose to the face of its master. "Leave me in peace! What's the matter, then?" At this point Brandis, as he lay on his back, looked upwards, then jumped up with a start and ran out into the bushes like one possessed. Pale as death, he arrived at the manor house with the news that there was a man hanging in the Jew's beech – he had seen the legs dangling just above his head.

"And you didn't cut him down, you fool?" cried the baron.

"Sir," panted Brandis, "if Your Lordship had been there, you would have known that the man was no longer alive. I thought, at first, it was the toadstools!"

Nevertheless, the squire urged his men to be quick and accompanied them himself.

They had arrived under the beech. "I can't see anything," said Herr von S***.

"You must stand here to see him... just here!"

It was just as Brandis had said: the squire recognized his own worn-out shoes. "My God, it's Johannes! Place the ladder against the tree... that's right... now bring him down... gently, gently! Don't let him fall! Good Heavens, the worms are already at work! But undo the noose and the cravat, just the same." A broad scar came into view; the squire started back. "Good gracious!" he said. He bent over the corpse again, looked at the scar intently and fell silent for a moment, deeply shaken. Then he turned to the foresters. "It is not right that the innocent should suffer for the guilty. Tell everybody that this man" – he pointed to the body – "was Friedrich Mergel." The corpse was buried in the carrion pit.

As far as all the main features are concerned, this really happened as I have related in September 1789. The Hebrew inscription on the tree means:

"If thou drawest nigh unto this place, it will befall thee as thou didst unto me."

Notes

p. 36, *Niemand*: "Nobody" (German).

p. 60, *the Feast of the Assumption*: The Assumption of Mary (the reception of the Virgin Mary into heaven, body and soul) is celebrated by the Roman Catholic Church on 15th August each year.

p. 69, *a "tabernacle for the sun"*: See Psalms 19:4–5.

p. 72, "In the beginning was the Word... and the Word was God": John 1:1.

p. 74, *"An eye for an eye, a tooth for a tooth!"*: Exodus 21:24.

p. 81, *Le vrai n'est pas toujours vraisemblable*: "Truth is not always plausible" (French).

101-PAGE CLASSICS

Great Rediscovered Classics

This series has been created with the aim to redefine and enrich the classics canon by promoting unjustly neglected works of enduring significance. These works, beautifully produced and mostly in translation, will intrigue and inspire the literary connoisseur and the general reader alike.

THE PERFECT COLLECTION OF LESSER-KNOWN WORKS BY MAJOR AUTHORS

almabooks.com/101-pages

On the Origin of Species, Charles Darwin
 Daniel Defoe, Moll Flanders
 Charles Dickens, A Christmas Carol
 David Copperfield, Charles Dickens
 Great Expectations, Charles Dickens
 Hard Times, Charles Dickens

 Charles Dickens, Oliver Twist
 Charles Dickens, A Tale of Two Cities
 The Double, Fyodor Dostoevsky
 Fyodor Dostoevsky, The Gambler
 The Idiot, Fyodor Dostoevsky
 Notes from Underground, Fyodor Dostoevsky

 Middlemarch, George Eliot
 The Mill on the Floss, George Eliot
 Praise of Folly, Erasmus
 The Beautiful and Damned, F. Scott Fitzgerald
 The Great Gatsby, F. Scott Fitzgerald
 Tender is the Night, F. Scott Fitzgerald

 Gustave Flaubert, Madame Bovary
 North and South, Elizabeth Gaskell
 The Sorrows of Young Werther, Goethe
 Dead Souls, Nikolai Gogol
 Nikolai Gogol, Petersburg Tales
 Thomas Hardy, Far from the Madding Crowd

 Thomas Hardy, Jude the Obscure
 Thomas Hardy, Tess of the D'Urbervilles
 Nathaniel Hawthorne, The Scarlet Letter
 The Portrait of a Lady, Henry James
 Three Men in a Boat, Jerome K. Jerome
 Dubliners, James Joyce

 Ulysses, James Joyce
 Franz Kafka, Metamorphosis
 Franz Kafka, The Trial
 Lady Chatterley's Lover, D.H. Lawrence
 Sons and Lovers, D.H. Lawrence
 Mikhail Lermontov, A Hero of Our Time

ALMA CLASSICS

ALMA CLASSICS aims to publish mainstream and lesser-known European classics in an innovative and striking way, while employing the highest editorial and production standards. By way of a unique approach the range offers much more, both visually and textually, than readers have come to expect from contemporary classics publishing.

LATEST TITLES PUBLISHED BY ALMA CLASSICS

www.almaclassics.com

For our complete list and latest offers

visit

almabooks.com/evergreens